THE RABBIT IN THE MOON

THE RABBIT

IN THE MOON

DHARMA PUBLISHING

© 1989 by Dharma Publishing USA. All rights reserved.
No part of this book may be reproduced in any form
without the publisher's written permission.

Story adapted by Dharma Publishing editorial staff.
Illustrated by Rosalyn White.
Color design by Julia Wittwer.
Printed in the USA by Dharma Press, 1241 21st Street,
Oakland, California 94607

Library of Congress Cataloging in Publication Data
will be found at the end of this book.

Dedicated to

children everywhere

The Jataka Tales

The Jataka Tales celebrate the power of action motivated by compassion, love, wisdom, and kindness. They teach that all we think and do profoundly affects the quality of our lives. Selfish words and deeds bring suffering to us and to those around us while selfless action gives rise to goodness of such power that it spreads in ever-widening circles, uplifting all forms of life.

The Jataka Tales, first related by the Buddha over two thousand years ago, bring to light his many lifetimes of positive action practiced for the sake of the world. As an embodiment of great compassion, the Awakened One reappears in many forms, in many times and places to ease the suffering of living beings. Thus these stories are filled with heroes of all kinds, each demonstrating the power of compassion and wisdom to transform any situation.

While based on traditional accounts, the stories in the Jataka Tales Series have been adapted for the children of today. May these tales inspire the positive action that will sustain the heart of goodness and the light of wisdom for the future of the world.

Tarthang Tulku   *Founder, Dharma Publishing*

Long ago in a faraway forest there once lived a Great Being in the form of a rabbit. All of the forest creatures considered this little rabbit their king. Though he was not as strong as the elephant nor as bold as the lion, he possessed the kindest of hearts. Everything the rabbit did, every word he spoke arose from friendliness. Feeling only love for others, he had never been afraid for himself. His heart was so pure that even the meanest, most frightening animals became his friends.

Three animals, an otter, a wolf, and a monkey, had come to regard the rabbit as their best friend. All day long they followed after him, wanting to see him and to hear him speak. Their love and admiration had even begun to change their animal natures. The greedy otter had learned to share with others, just as the rabbit did; the sly wolf no longer thought of stealing, and the mischievous monkey had completely forgotten how to tease.

People were filled with wonder at this remarkable change, for they did not understand the great power of kindness. Even Shakra, king of heavenly beings, was perplexed as he watched the little rabbit and his friends in the forest.

One evening the rabbit, the otter, the wolf, and the monkey were lying on the soft cool grass in a clearing of the forest filled with the light of the moon.

"See how the beautiful moon is nearly full!" exclaimed the rabbit. As he gazed up at the silver mirror in the dark sky, he told his friends his thoughts. "The full moon is the best time for good deeds! Just as moonlight clears away darkness, goodness removes all evil and unhappiness. Let us think of how we can bring happiness to whoever might visit the forest tomorrow."

But long after the otter, the wolf, and the monkey had fallen asleep, the rabbit was still thinking very hard. "My only food is blades of green grass, which most creatures do not enjoy. My only warmth is my fur coat which I cannot give another. What could I offer a guest on the full moon? How helpless I am! I must think of something." And all night long the rabbit gazed up at the moon and thought and thought.

The noble wishes of the rabbit and his friends made Shakra sit up straight on his throne, for such concern for others on the part of animals was rare indeed. "I must go into this forest myself to test their resolve. Are their actions true to their speech?"

The next afternoon when the forest creatures were seeking out cool shadows and hiding away amongst the leafiest trees, Shakra stepped into the clearing disguised as an old man. Weeping and wailing, he perfectly imitated a traveler who had lost his way, weary with hunger and thirst, distress and worry.

"Ah me! I am lost and alone. Who shall ever find me? I will surely starve to death here in this woods. Ah me!"

The four friends, alarmed by such pitiful sounds, hurried to the side of the old man to comfort him. "Do not be afraid. We are your friends and will help you in every way we can. Please, please, sit down and we shall try to make you comfortable."

The otter ran quickly off and returned with seven fish. "Some forgetful fisherman left these by the lake. Please eat them for they will give you strength. I used to be very greedy, so I know what is good to eat."

"And here," said the wolf, "is a pail of milk someone left in the forest. It will help you sleep, and as you rest, I will be your guard. I used to be sneaky and sly, so I am good at keeping watch."

Then the monkey brought ripe mangoes that were perfectly round and colored deep orange. "Refresh yourself and in the morning, I will find a way out of the forest. I used to play tricks on everyone, so I am good at being clever."

Finally the rabbit came forward and spoke to the old man. "I am but a rabbit who has grown up in this forest. I have nothing to offer to such a deserving guest. If you will but build a fire, I will try to find something delicious for you to cook."

The old man snapped his fingers and a huge blazing fire sprang up in the clearing, flickering golden flames and sending sparks in all directions.

Suddenly, the rabbit knew what he could give. Filled with joy, he bowed to the old man and said, "My heart insists on giving, and I know now what I might offer. Fulfill my wishes and feast upon me!" And he leaped toward the blazing fire.

At that very moment, the king of heavenly beings reached out his long and beautiful hands, caught the little rabbit, and lifted him up into the sky.

"Behold and rejoice at this astonishing deed! When most cannot give up even faded flowers without misgivings, this one offers his own body without hesitation. How lofty and shining is his heart, like the disk of the full moon."

Then in order to remind the world of the power of selfless-ness, he placed the rabbit in the moon, where he has dwelt from that day forward. Every month when the moon is full, the shape of the rabbit with the pure heart can be seen in the silvery moon.

The Jataka Tales Series

Library of Congress Cataloging in Publication Data

The Rabbit in the moon.

   (Jataka tales series)
   Based on a tale from the Jatakas.
   Summary: Rabbit's unselfish deed of offering himself
for food to a hungry stranger is rewarded when he is
placed in the moon for all to see.
   1. Jataka stories, English.   [1. Jataka stories]
I. White, Rosalyn, ill.   II. Series.
BQ1462.E5R33   1989   294.3'823   88–33456
ISBN 0–89800–190–0
ISBN 0–89800–191–9 (pbk.)

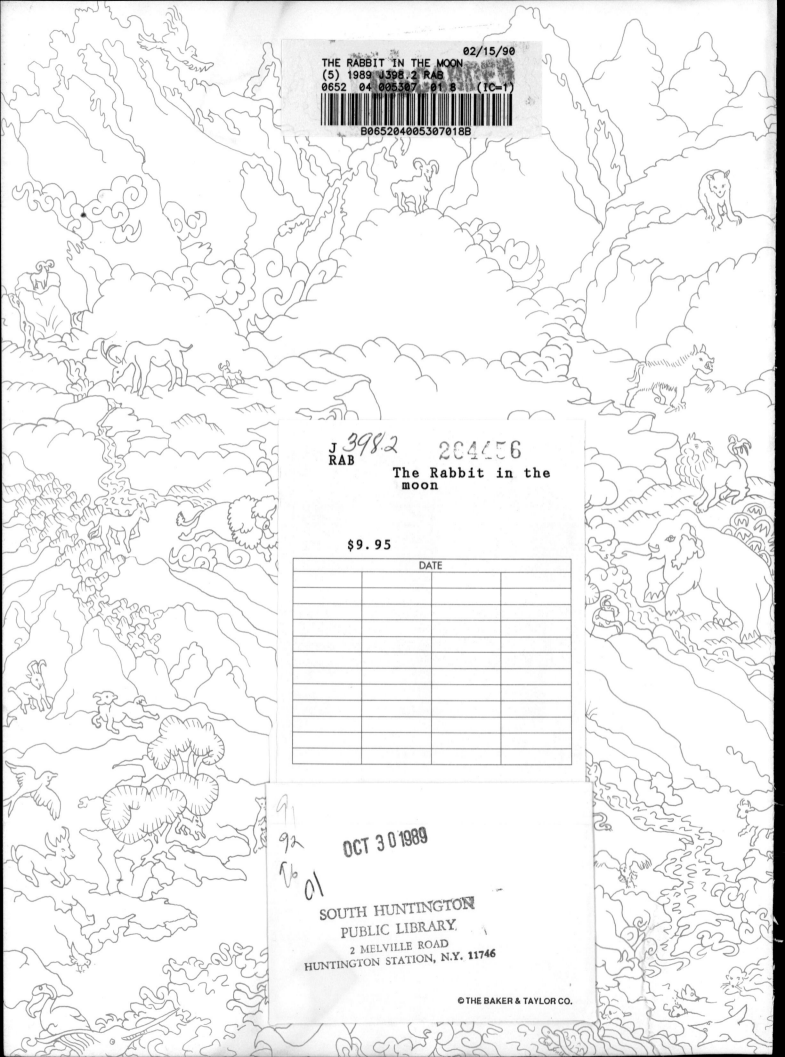